HAUNTED LOVE STORIES

Aunt Elsie's Dime Store Romance Series

by

Zia Narella

illustrated by

Vikki Chu

DARKER INTENTIONS PRESS

Published by
DARKER INTENTIONS PRESS
POB 569
Freehold Township, New Jersey 07728-0569

Printed in the United States of America

ISBN: 0976961245

For more information on Darker Intentions Press, please visit us on the Web at: www.darkerintentionspress.com or contact jzdakota@hotmail.com

Illustrated by Vikki Chu
Back cover design and layout by Dariusz Golen

THE LADY IN WHITE
MEETS HER MATCH

"Like some tired, played-out rock band, it's just another night on the road."

Every night it's the same tired routine along a treacherous stretch of highway. If I walk that strip at midnight one more time, I think I'm going to kill myself. But the problem is, I'm already dead.

My name was Helen Worth. I died in a car accident along Route 17 in Tuxedo, New York in June of 1977, the eve of my high school prom. I'm buried in Heavenly Rest, a small cemetery located a few miles off the highway. Since then, it's been the same tedious routine, every single midnight. I rise from my grave, walk the roadway, and wait for some living fool to drive by and pick me up.

Nothing's changed, not even my clothes. I wear the same long white cotton dress, with a fitted waist and a lace up peasant blouse front. My grandmother's Whiting and Davis purse swings from right hand, while my left hand still carries the single red rose Dad gave me the night I left my house. I will never forget how excited I was!

It was a magical night. I didn't have a date, but my girl-friend's brother had a best friend who offered to take me to my prom. He told Laurie's brother that he'd always thought I was cute, but never had the nerve to ask me out. I decided to chance it and hoped that my mystery date wasn't a troll who expected a French kiss at the end of the night. Blech!

That evening the limousine was supposed to pick me, Laurie, mystery date, and Laurie's brother up at Laurie's house. From there we would make our debut at Wakely High School Auditorium at 8: 00 pm. By the end of the night, I would have my arms wrapped around my date to the tune of Abba's "Dancing Queen." It was kind of a corny song, but probably less provocative than Foreigner's "Feels Like the First Time." This was my night and it was going to be a great, great party.

My fate changed when a single car on a two lane stretch of Route 17 struck mine head on, killing me instantly. I never made it to Laurie's house, let alone my prom, and while I was buried in a completely different dress, I wound up eternally stuck in my prom gown. The last thing I remember were headlights, screaming my head off, and watching my friends crying at my wake as I hovered in a distant corner of the viewing room of Mortelamour's Funeral Parlor. But what bothered me the most is that I never got to the prom, my prom. So now it's 2006 and for twenty nine years, I've been walking alone on this road, not doing much of anything except getting into cars driven by the living. Each time I do it, it's the same routine.

A car pulls alongside the road. I drift over, stick my head in the window, and ask for a ride. Ironically, if the driver were to look at me from behind, he would see that I'm elevated several inches off the ground. But leaning in the car window, I look pretty human—for the moment. I throw my purse and flower on the back seat and hop in. The conversation is always dull and usually goes like this:

"Where are you going?"

"Just down the road." I whisper softly.

"Too late for a pretty girl like you to be out and about."

Yeah fool, I've only been a corpse for twenty nine years. I think to myself, but I'm polite anyway.

" It's okay. I love the night air."

"Got a name?"

"Helen. Can you take me to 69 Franklin Street in Tuxedo?"

"Sure. Past Heavenly Rest Cemetery?"

I smile. "Yes, that's exactly the place."

The non-dead driver, usually a guy in his twenties, chatters away about what's happening in his life. That's how I keep up with what the living are up to, since we don't exactly have newspapers or the internet here in the dead zone. I've ridden in brand new Nissans, a couple of Honda Accords, a Mercedes, and a vintage 1975 Eldorado. I've learned all about movies made in 1984 like "Ghostbusters," and the 2006 remake of "The Omen." I've also heard that

I am now an urban legend, and that there are several of us 'Ladies in White' spotted across the country. I've driven with drunken drivers, an experience not recommended for the living unless you want to end up like me, and perverts who tried to grab me way above the ankle, only to wind up with a handful of air. Either way, I get them to pull alongside the road in front of Heavenly Rest. I turn to them smile, and watch the looks of horror on their faces as I swan dive back into my grave right before their eyes with a Banshee-like howl. I make sure to leave my rose and purse on the seat, which usually vanish during twilight hours.

Tonight will be the same damn thing. Like some tired, played-out rock band, it's just another night on the road.

I walk along the shoulder. I see a car pull up. Interesting. This time it's a '69 Buick Le Sabre, so I figure it's just some antique car hound. I walk over to the window and I hear the Buick's window straining as he rolls it down. I look in the car at the driver.

"You look exhausted, pretty lady."

"What?" *Of course, I look exhausted, I'm dead.* I couldn't help but notice that for a living guy, he was different than the guys I was used to. He kinda reminded me of a young Jackson Brown with his hairstyle and smile, a truly handsome *living* man. Now this was really going to cramp my nightly haunting routine. I haven't been attracted to a living man in decades, and for some reason I didn't want to frighten this one.

"I said you look tired. Hop in and I'll give you a lift."

"Okay." I threw the rose and purse on the back seat. We drove with neither of us speaking a word. This was unusual. I couldn't take it, so I broke the silence.

"What's your name?"

"Andrew. But my friends used to call me Andy. So where are you going?"

"Just up the road to 69 Franklin Street. It's where I used to live."

Andy looked at my face and I felt his eyes go right through me. "*Used* to live?" he asked. "If you don't live there anymore, why

"Just up the road to 69 Franklin Street. It's where I used to live."

do you want me to drive you to that address?"

"Well, actually you can drop me off slightly before there."

"Okay, but I have to make little detour before I take you home."

"Sure, whatever." I smell, really smell, the scent of his leather jacket and it arouses me. I remember getting this feeling that I had as a young girl. I think it was physical attraction, which makes no sense since I don't own a physical body anymore. Well, I do but it's rotting inside a coffin a few miles away. "So, uh, what do you do for a living, Andy?"

"That's s good way of putting it. Let's just say, I'm a driver. Oh, we're getting close to my place."

Andy pulls the Buick up alongside of Hillside Cemetery, a non-sectarian burial place. He turns the engine off. I laugh to myself because if he thinks he's going to get any action, I can just vanish into thin air. Although part of me really wants to touch him.

"So why are we stopping here? I mean this is, like a graveyard."

He laughed. "Yes, yes it is." At that point, the doors on the Buick locked by themselves.

That's funny. I don't remember this model having power locks. I think to myself. *This is flipping me out. I better vanish out of here.* Too nervous to look at Mr. Leather Jacket, I close my eyes, and try my vanishing routine and only to find that I'm not going anywhere. I open my eyes and I'm still stuck inside the Buick. I reach for the door handle. It doesn't budge. Then I do what any stupid living 17 year old girl does. I started pounding on the windows with my hands.

"Hel-l-lp me! Somebody help me!" I make a fist and try to punch out the window. Nothing happens. Then I felt a warm hand on my shoulder. It was Andy's.

"Helen, I think we should talk."

"You know me?"

"Yes, though we've never met. My name is Andrew Woods. I was Laurie's brother's best friend. I was supposed to take you to the prom, but then you were in an accident. Do you remember anything about it?"

I'm a ghost. The worse thing a ghost can do is remember its earthly life, which is what ties me to the highway. "All I remember is that some jerk hit me head on and the next thing I know is that I'm laying in a pine box and walking this highway every night."

"Helen, I'm the jerk that killed you."

With a knee-jerk, no pun intended, response I slap him across the face. I feel heat, the roughness of a man's after five shadow, and twenty nine years of anger. "You creep! You ruined my life and now you're even ruining my death. Go away!" I felt hot tears running down my face. My usually pristine prom hairstyle collapsed. My mascara ran. In a word, I was a ghostly, ghastly mess.

Andy brushed my hair off my face. "Helen, please don't cry. What have I done? May be I should have left you alone." He took in a deep breath. "Helen, do your remember anything else about that night?"

"No. I don't." I sobbed. Looking in my purse, I found a nice moldy twenty nine year old hankerchief and wiped my eyes.

"Look, there's something you should know. I died that night, too."

"You mean you're n-not, alive?"

"No, Helen, I'm dead." He took my face in his strong hands, placed his lips over mine and gave me a deep hard kiss. I tried to pull away at first, but then I realized that I enjoyed his touch too much. "And I've been searching up and down this highway, giving rides to living women trying to find out if anyone knew anything about you. I wanted to tell you how sorry I was for hurting you. I never meant anyone any harm."

"Thank you." I felt alive again. But this wasn't possible, I was dead. "You know, Andy if we were living, I think we'd be closing in on fifty years old."

"Wait, I can do that." Suddenly Andy morphed into this really stunning looking older man. "We can be seventeen or forty-six. What do you want to do?"

I looked at the Hillside cemetery and then thought of Heavenly Rest. "Well, my graveyard or yours?"

"Heavenly Rest has a better view." Before Andy cranked up the engine, he shoved an eight track into his tape player, and "Walk this Way" by Aerosmith came blasting out of the speakers, as he hit the gas pedal. We burned rubber vanishing into the night air. It was early and we ghosts had a lot of catching up to do before sunrise.

JULIAN'S WOODS

I was always one number short on the lottery, one day late to discover the idea that would revolutionize modern society. And as if the Fates weren't unkind enough, I was also unlucky in love. When I was notified that I had inherited my grandmother's working farm in Cranbury, New Jersey I thought things would be different because my luck was changing. Cranbury Farm came complete with horses, two hundred acres, and servants. It was all that I could have wished for.

Out of all the cousins and uncles, nieces and nephews, Gramma chose to leave Cranbury Farm to me. Why? I hadn't seen her since I was a child. She wrote to me over the years, but her letters were strange, and at times nonsensical. I blamed old age as the reason why she wrote about events of the past and people long dead. Over the years, Gramma had become a hermit, and I seemed to be following her footsteps.

I recall being at the farm a few times in my youth. I never went there directly. My parents and I always seemed to be visiting someone else and then I would bicycle over to Gramma's place, much to the annoyance of my parents. I often got the feeling they wanted me to stay away from Cranbury Farm, though I never understood why.

Once I arrived I'd find Gramma in the kitchen. She would just talk and talk and I would listen. But I remember her saying to me when I was little, "Once you grow up, Georgina, the farm will be lonely. It will have no friends. It needs you. Maybe someday I just might give it to you." When I asked her why she thought the farm would be lonely, Gramma never really explained it.

"You, my pretty Miss Georgina Blanchard, will know soon enough. But sometimes you shouldn't ask. Accept life's good lessons as they come."

Miss Georgina Blanchard. Oh how, I hated the *Miss* part!

It reminded me of a silly card game I played as a little girl—Old Maid. No one ever wanted to win *that* card, even though she was always depicted as a sweet faced old gal. Now like the Old Maid, I was the last single card in the Blanchard family deck, destined for a life of spinsterhood. I could hear the voices of my nieces and nephews calling me, "dear old Aunt Georgie," or my obituary describing me as "the maiden Aunt Blanchard." Maybe this is why Gramma gave me that farm. It was as a substitute for a portion of my life that would forever remain empty.

When the County Surrogate mailed me a copy of Gramma Ida Mae Blanchard's will, the will had a strange request in it. If at any point in time, I failed to obey her post mortem directive, I would be forced to leave the farm immediately. The request had to do with the care of her farm workers.

Cranbury Farm maintained a staff of six people since the 1950's. There was a housekeeper, a horse handler, a landscaper and his family and an old farm hand. Every night at six o'clock, my grandmother served an evening meal to the little party. When the meal was complete, Gramma proceeded to clear the table and do the dishes. Now that she had passed on, the will demanded that I clear the dinner table dishes each night when the meal was over.

I often wondered who would throw me off the farm if I disobeyed Gramma's wishes, but I decided it was easier to cooperate than to cause trouble and find out.

#

The day came when I pulled up in my car to Cranbury Farm with a moving truck trailing behind me. As I stepped from the car, a short, cherubic Irishwoman waited for me.

"Well, hello there! You must be Miss Georgina. I am Mrs. McCarthy, I worked for your Gramma, dear, dear Ida Mae. I miss her terribly. She was a lovely soul."

Mrs. McCarthy struck a tender cord within me. She reminded of all good childhood memories, vanilla spice and warm apple pies in the oven.

"We have just a few rules here and there. If you ever need anything, please don't hesitate to ask. Just call me and I will be there in a minute. Now let me introduce you to the others. You know the rule about the evening meal, yes?"

"You mean clearing the dinner dishes? Yes, I know. Why was that so important to Gramma Ida Mae?"

"Oh, it was just something she did that she thought was good manners, I suppose." Mrs. McCarthy took me by the hand and walked me around the farm. "Very little has changed here since the 1950's other than updating the plumbing and electricity. Mr. Oakes! Mr. Oakes! Get down from your tractor! Come and meet the new Lady of Cranbury Farm!"

A gentleman stepped down from the tractor, and removed a straw hat. Like Mrs. McCarthy, I saw he wasn't young, but I couldn't hazard a guess at his age. His overalls were worn and dirty. The man's cheeks were pink and youthful, yet his face had a thousand crevasses. It was the face of a man who'd lived a hard life. When I looked at Mr. Oakes, a melancholy presence came over me, even though he had striking eyes that were robin egg blue. He slowly extended a hand, forced a smile and said, "Welcome. If you need anything, anything at all, please let me know."

"Nice to meet you, Mr. Oakes. Mrs. McCarthy, is Mr. Oakes responsible for all the beautiful flowers around the farm?"

"No dear," she giggled. "Here they come now. You can thank the florists yourself."

A family slowly walked down the road through the entrance gate of Cranbury Farm. Like Mr. Oakes, the father wore the same straw hat. His wife was dressed in a colorful embroidered dress. Holding her hand was a young barefoot little boy. He handed me a basket of fresh cut flowers.

Remembering a course in high school Spanish, I responded, *"Muchas gracias. Como te llamas?"*

The little boy gave me a wide smile. *"Me llamo es Joseba Sanchez."*

"Now that Gramma passed on, the will demanded that I clear the
dinner table dishes when the meal was over."

"So Joseba, how long have you been at the farm?" Joseba looked at his father for an answer.

Mr. Sanchez piped up with broken English. "Many, many years, we are here. My family and I come from Mexico. I grow flower, many, many flower there. Much better to grow flower here. Better life here." He sighed. Mr. Sanchez, like Mr. Oakes and Mrs. McCarthy before him repeated the strange mantra: if I ever needed anything, please let them know.

And like Mr. Oakes and Mrs. McCarthy, the Sanchez family had an eerie feling surrounding them. It was the quiet dignity of a well maintained graveyard, peaceful, yet still a place of mourning, a place people like to stay for a very long.

"Is that the entire staff, Mrs. McCarthy?"

She smiled. "Funny you should inquire, my dear. There is still one more person. Follow me."

She took me by the hand again, and lead me out to the barn where an impatient gelding stood in cross ties. A few feet away from him, I saw the back of a farrier leaning over the flames of a forge. Sparks flew each time he struck the horseshoe lying on his anvil, manipulating what appeared to me as the power of Vulcan.

The heat took my breath away. When he had finished the final blow to the horseshoe, he dropped it into a cauldron. The water cracked and sizzled, causing clouds of steam to rise and become a barrier between us. Over the rising mist of the cauldron, I caught his glance. And he looked at me…strangely.

His short fiery auburn hair was wet with sweat and steam. He had remarkably piercing gray eyes. His shoulders were broad, with well defined muscular arms. His features were not aqualine or chiseled, and his face had a certain rugged edge to it. I noticed that he was not young, but like the other people at the farm, there was this aura about him that defied description.

"So this is the new lady of Cranbury Farm," he said with an effusive bow. "Welcome. If there is anything you need..."

"Yes. Don't hesistate to ask."

"You get the picture, then? I am Julian Jamison, farrier,

horse trainer..."

"And musician," interjected Mrs. McCarthy. "Don't forget musician. A very fine classical musician."

"That's wonderful, Julian. What do you play?"

"You'll find out, soon. It really isn't important, now." He turned away. Then he changed the subject. "Listen, do you ride? Ida Mae's horses were sound and well trained. They are also re-markably quiet. If you want to go riding or carriage driving, let me know. I'll get one of the nags ready for you." The horse in the cross ties whinnied impatiently as Julian extended his hand. "Welcome, Miss Georgina. It is good to have you back at Cranbury Farm. I bet-ter finish shoeing him. My boy, Middleburg, gets a little ancy if he's tied up too long."

I nodded and smiled as Mrs. McCarthy lead me back to the main farm house. At that moment I realized that I never told Julian my name. I hadn't been back to the farm in decades.

#

Keeping true to my grandmother's wishes, I went to the bunk house dining room every night, cleared the table, and washed the dinner dishes. The food was barely eaten, and I always threw away more food than the workers ate.

One clear August night I left my bedroom window open. The day had been unusually hot, but it had rained and by nightfall, there was a cool breeze. I opened my bedroom window. Traveling on the wind was the sound of a beautiful yet mournful cello. I rec-ognized the tune. It was "Nina" by Pergolese, a 17th century Italian musician.

It drew me to Julian. I felt the urge to go to him, but I knew it would be better to resist. I was lonely, but not an easy mark—at least for now. Gramma's farm was a strange place and becoming more peculiar by the moment. Though the music called to me, I simply shut the window and went to sleep.

Many peaceful months passed at Cranbury Farm. My stay

"Traveling on the wind was the sound of a beautiful yet mournful cello."

there seemed like a pleasant, sweet dream. Julian and I had developed a warm friendship, the kind a man and a woman have when they are on the verge of perhaps becoming lovers. We were both extremely attracted to each other, and I thought there was a time when I saw him blush as he looked in my direction. Julian was a bit of a rough cut, but yet there was something gentle about him, at least when he spoke to me.

He would do anything for me. All I had to do was make mention of my desire to ride or drive, and I would find the animal fully tacked or the carriage hooked up and ready to go. But it was odd. When I arrived at the barn, the horse was always ready but Julian was nowhere to be found.

Then into the forest I would go. My horse in a steady rhythmic canter, the smell of the pine, and songs of the birds lured me deeper and deeper into the woods. Even though I was the owner of the land, in my heart I knew the forest would always belong to Gramma Ida Mae. This was her sacred space. And I didn't realize that her presence was there more than I could possibly imagine.

Today I rode River, a draft quarterhorse gelding. I'd been out in the woods for about an hour, before I was overcome with a feeling of exhaustion. Being tired and on a big horse, isn't safe, so I decided to head back to the main house and have a nap before dinner.

I turned the horse's head and used a little leg pressure to move him forward. As I squeezed his barrel, the horse yanked the reins from my hand. River flatly refused to head into the direction I wanted him to go, and threw a large buck. I grabbed a hunk of mane hanging on for dear life. I lost control and River reared straight up in the air.

Julian appeared from out of nowhere. Strong arms grabbed the reins. Seconds later, River calmed down and became peaceful once again.

"What's the matter with you? What were you told about going into this part of the woods?"

"I don't know what you mean." Then I bristled. "Who the

hell are you to tell me what to do? I own the woods not you!"

He grabbed me and pulled me off the horse's back. "You may own the woods, but *I* own the night." Then he kissed me. My knees grew weak. I felt faint and dizzy. The last thing I remember was soft cello music playing in the background. But this would have been impossible. We were out in the middle of a forest.

#

When I awoke the next morning, I found myself sprawled across a bed in my night gown. My head was killing me. It was as though a thousand Swiss bell ringers were locked inside my cerebellum trying to hammer their way out through my ears, a hangover without cheap wine as the reason. As I lay awake with my head throbbing, a cheerful knock at the bedroom door from Mrs. McCarthy with french toast and eggs was hardly on my agenda.

"Well, my pretty Miss! You certainly gave Julian and I a good scare."

I was still dumbstruck. "Wh-what happened?"

"Well, River spooked and dropped you on your head."

"Dropped me on my head? I thought my mother did that when I was five."

"Well Georgina, history repeated itself. You should never ride in that part of the woods alone."

"Why?"

"You weren't headed toward the site of the old cemetery were you?"

"I have no idea. I was riding. What old cemetery?"

"Nothing dear, don't give it a second thought." Mrs. McCarthy's eyes looked away. "There's just an old cemetery on the back of the property. Vagrants have been known to sleep there. That's why it's dangerous, my dear. Julian and Mr. Sanchez will often go out there and chase them away. Squatters, I suspect."

"How did I get back here?"

"Easy enough. River came back alone. An empty saddle is

17

always a sign of a rider down. Julian went to fetch you. Well, must get back to work, now. Will you be available tonight to clear the dinner dishes?"

Before I could respond, the little woman dashed from room. I wasn't satisfied with her answers or her questions. What was the deal with the cemetery? And why was she so concerned about the dinner dishes? None of this made sense to me. I bolted out of the bed and looked out the door to the end of hallway. Mrs. McCarthy was nowhere to be found. But someone else was.

"Quite a fall you took. Old River's never spooked like that before." Julian had a certain merriment in his eyes, a merriment I didn't care for.

"Look, I know what happened. The horse didn't dump me and I didn't fall on my head. You, you must have drugged me or something."

"I don't think so."

"How did I get back here?"

"I carried you. No easy task, I assure you."

"What's going on? You tell me!"

"Calm down."

"Don't tell me to calm down. I'm not going to calm down. Why didn't you explain about the vagrants and the graveyard? Why all the mystery?"

His face paled over a bit. "You know about the graveyard?"

"Yes. Mrs. McCarthy told me about you and Sanchez going out there chasing away vagrants. I thought homeless people sleeping in a cemetery was distinctly a city phenomenon."

"Well, it's a rural one, too." He rubbed his chin. "Forget the cemetery for a minute. Would you like to have dinner tonight at my cottage?"

"So how do I know you aren't a serial killer? Something weird happened out there yesterday."

He sighed sadly. "Nothing weird happened, Georgina. You fell from your horse, and were nearly unconscious. I thought we were going to have to take you to the hospital. Just forget about the woods for a minute. What about dinner?"

"So I suppose you skip dinner with crew and we'll eat at six?"

"No, I have to eat with them. You and I will eat at seven, after you clear the dinner dishes, of course."

"Julian, what's with this dinner thing? I have an idea. Let's get off the farm and eat at the Cranbury Inn. My treat."

The happiness left Julian's eyes. His face clouded over. "No, I can't do that. Look, just drop by about seven thirty." He reached out a hand and touched my cheek. "You will come, won't you?"

"Yes, Julian I will."

I didn't know why, but I would go to him. It was where my heart wanted to be.

#

I had just finished clearing the dinner dishes when I heard the cello music. Julian was playing "Nina" again, that haunting beautiful melody. I followed the music to his cottage.

I didn't have to knock. With the touch of a fingertip, the wooden cottage door opened and I saw a small dinner table set for two. He invited me to his table, and we dined. I don't remember what Julian and I ate; I think I spent to much time gazing into his eyes. And when we finally made love for the second time, I caught a glimpse of his soul but he made me make a solemn promise.

"Georgina, you have to do something for me."

"Don't ever go out into that section of the woods again. It's dangerous."

"Why? Because of a bunch of drunken squatters?"

"Look. Just don't do it. I'd hate to see something happen to you. Georgina, do you think that you could be happy spending the rest of your life with me at Cranbury Farm?"

"Julian, I love it here. But it's strange. I took time off from work to settle in. But I'm the kind of gal that likes to come and go. I feel like no one ever goes off the farm. Don't you ever want to leave

19

this place once and awhile? See something different, maybe?"

He smiled. "I used to. But that was another life time ago."

"So how long have you been on the farm?"

"Oh, the better part of twenty years. But things happen. I've seen a lot in the world and I like the solitude. Don't have much for people anymore." He placed his hands on my shoulders. "Your life could be so comfortable here. You'd never need to leave the place. Do you feel mistreated here?"

"Of course not. But I just can't stay on the farm twenty four seven."

When I made this statement, he jokingly pinned back my arms and placed his naked body on top of mine with an air of joyful defiance. Then he whispered into my ear as he kissed my neck. "You won't stay even for the sake of my music?"

I laughed and touched his cheek. "Well, I *suppose* I could make an exception."

#

The days were growing short. When I arrived home, the Sanchez family, Mr. Oakes, Mrs. McCarthy and Julian were usually through with dinner and it was dark. By that time, the little troupe was nowhere to be found. It was a curious living arrangement, but I'd grown accustom to it. I tried to remember what Gramma Ida Mae said: never question a good thing. For the most part, I felt all of my needs were attended to by Gramma's staff. But the best part of living on Cranbury Farm was Julian.

Each day I was becoming more and more drawn to him. I was starting to love him. But it was difficult having a relationship with a man, who wouldn't discuss his past, and had no ideas about tomorrow. I wasn't twenty, anymore. The rules in the game of life are different when you get older. And it seemed that Julian didn't plan on getting older or married. He would often tell me his future was in his music, his horses and me. The time was now...and that gave him all the tomorrow he ever needed.

#

It all came to a head on a fateful Saturday afternoon, when I was in a local antique store. I was staring at a lovely old butter churn when the proprietor of the store came up to me.

"Dressy piece, isn't it? Can't do much about the smell though, that is why I am selling it at such an outrageous discount. I rescued it from the remnants of local farm that burned down in the 1950's."

"Really? I just moved into a local farm."

"Which one?"

"Cranbury Farm."

"You mean the old Blanchard place?"

I caught my breath. "You know the farm?"

"Sure. It was legendary around here. What a tragedy! Place burned down in 1952. Ida Mae Blanchard, the owner was rescued from the fire, but her help didn't make it. It was rumored that she went crazy and stayed there, living in that dump and serving a full course dinner for the dead every night. I hear she died awhile back and the place was abandoned. Was supposed to go up for public auction. Did you buy that place? It's gonna cost you a lot of money to get that place up and running. Ma'am, are you okay? Ma'am?"

I felt sick. "Excuse me, I've got to go."

#

I drove back to Cranbury Farm at breakneck speed. I ran into the barn and grabbed River, trying not to think of Julian. It didn't work. The moment I envisioned his face in my mind he appeared. I couldn't talk to him. Tears filled my eyes, and the horse I saddled started jigging around nervously. Julian looked at me.

"Can I get you something Georgina? Here let me help you."

"No!" I shrieked.

"What's the matter, love?"

21

"Get away from me." I tightened River's girth, hopped on his back and drove him straight into the woods, the part of the woods that was dangerous.

#

It seemed like we rode forever. I was alone in the woods and I didn't care. When we entered the clearing, River tried to rear up. I jammed my spurs into his barrel and drove him forward, fighting him every inch of the way. When I got close enough to where I wanted to be, I jumped off his back and he ran away. In front of me was the mystery of Gramma Ida Mae's woods.

They were covered by bramble, and some of their tops were broken off. I counted six tombstones in all, three in the front, and three in the back. The names were all there, Edwina McCarthy, Philip Oakes, Moraima and Octavio Sanchez, Joseba Sanchez and finally, Julian Jamison. This was the secret of Cranbury Farm.

A chill came over me. And then I felt a cool hand on my shoulder. It was Julian.

"So now you know. Why did you have to come out here, Georgina? Why? You'll have to leave the farm now. I guess that was Ida Mae's plan all along. I just didn't see it."

"What are you talking about?"

"You can't love me anymore, can you?"

"How can I love you? You're dead."

"I thought love was stronger than death. Your grandmother once told me what a fine woman you would grow up to be. She was right."

Behind Julian stood the rest of my Gramma's staff. As Mrs. McCarthy cried, Mr. Oakes rested a gentle hand on her shoulder. The Sanchez family stood quietly. Their little boy still had flowers in his hand. Very slowly, the group turned away and walked into the woods. Their images faded and then finally vanished. Julian remained a few moments longer.

"Things will be different for you now. Cranbury Farm was

"The dead cannot travel with the living."

a wonderful place when you were here, but you can't stay anymore and neither can I."

"So why did she leave me this place? Gramma should have taken here own advice. Look what happened to her after you all died. She was so guilt ridden she pretended to serve you dinner for decades. She stayed alone and it probably drove her mad. Was I supposed to be the next caretaker of the dead?"

"She felt that you stopped living. You were becoming like her and maybe you just didn't see it." His cool hand touched my face. "Good bye, my love."

A thunder clap broke and he was gone.

I stood in front of Cranbury Farm and saw the farm as it really was, a burned out shell with a dilapidated cottage next to it. Any flowers were dead and long gone. The stable was a bunch of half burned, broken boards. From all outward appearances, there hadn't been a living thing in the place for decades. The air surrounding Cranbury Farm smelled of age, fire and death.

Where had I been for the past six months? I was too confused and too terrified to answer my own question. But Julian was right. The dead cannot travel with the living. My past was over and it was time to look to the future.

THE DARK HORSEMAN

MIDNIGHT
PAIMPONT, FRANCE

The tiny village nestled deeply in the forest of Paimpont made her home seem like an almost impossible destination. As he drove his horses through the Breton countryside under the cover of moonlight, he sighed. These tedious little French villages were all the same. Quite frankly, the scenery which so often fascinated the English bored him, particularly at night.

And he wasn't traveling at this hour as some itinerant merchant, no, no.

Tonight he journeyed the dark woods because a beautiful woman waited for him.

He must reach her because it was their destiny to end up together. Time was always on his side. After all, this woman wanted him for so long. In fact, she yearned for him years ago, but the time was never right for their union. Now, time and fate were perfectly aligned. He rushed to her bed without hesitation.

As the horseman tilted his head back, he sniffed the night air.

Yes, he thought. *Yes, it is Renee.* He inhaled again. *Ren-nee. It is time for my Renee.*

Her essence commingled with the wind in the trees. It was an earthy fragrance, a mixture of sweat, lavender, and sweet grass, the smell of a peasant woman. It aroused him. Most of the noblewomen the horseman made love to preferred masking their bodies in pungent Oriental oils. But his woman's scent was different. It exuded sex and called to him. Her aura was wonderful! In an age where he frequently smelled gangrenous flesh or chamber pots, sweet grass and lavender made the wearer an exquisite delight for him.

"Alain, c'est toi?"

How shall I take her? he pondered.

Perhaps he would caress her gently, tenderly joining his body with hers for a full union of the flesh and spirit. Maybe he would simply grind himself into her, furiously pounding away at her body the way the sea crashes against the shore in a relentless thunderstorm. As he played with these thoughts as he tried to remember if her eyes were blue or a muddy hazel. Finally, he stopped thinking. It was just too much excitement, even for a rogue like him.

The wagon's wheels creaked rhythmically as they passed over the soil. Renee's fragrance grew stronger as he grew closer to his destination. He cracked his driving whip against the horses' rumps. They responded by moving from a working trot into a steady and deliberate canter. In the far distance, he saw the light from her cottage shining through a small window. Ah, sweet destiny, he was nearly there!

He didn't want to be seen by anyone, so he stopped his wagon a few hundred feet from the thatched-roof cottage. Ever patient and observant, the horseman studied the movement within the house. Squinting, he saw the glow of a dying fire reflecting shadows of expressionless figures milling about the hearth. He sensed a certain sadness, but the horseman had no idea why these people were unhappy. This was a momentous occasion, at least in his eyes. He dismounted from his cart and peered into the window of her boudoir.

Renee's bedroom resembled a closet attached to a cramped parlor where the rest of her family paced nervously. He wondered if he should enter the tiny dwelling house through the door or the shuttered window. Wearing his cloak and hat, he could make a magnificent sweeping entrance. If he went through the window, he would be forced to collapse his massive form quite a bit to fit through such a small space, even though he could do it with ease.

Door or window, door or window? he quietly questioned. *Window, yes, yes, that's it.* He would make his entry through the window to capture his woman.

Long fingers delicately opened the shutters. Quietly, he

slipped into her bedroom unnoticed by her family in the next room. She laid upon a thin mattress. Her eyes, which usually fluttered in and out of a dreamless sleep, suddenly opened wide. She smiled at the sight of him.

"Alain, c'est toi?"

"Yes, Renee. It's me."

"It has been so long, so late. Why do you come now?"

"Par amour, Renee. Parce que je t'aime." He touched her cheek. "Love is never too late."

"Is that so?"

She was the same vibrant young woman he remembered years ago when they nearly collided in a carriage accident. Oh, he had to let her get away then, but now he had her back.

Gently, he removed her night dress, letting it fall effortlessly to the ground. With his thin hands, her lover brushed her hair from her face. The soft fragile wisps became a long blond mane, caressing her shoulders as it had done so many times before. He removed his cloak and hat as he joined her in her nakedness.

He began to kiss her, slowly at first, but he found he had little restraint when Renee was near him. Moments later, he found himself within her, deep within her, and he knew that she still believed in him. This act of passion was what she wanted so many decades ago. Her muffled moans betrayed desire fulfilled.

When he was finished, he looked at the woman lying silently beneath him. He smiled to himself, complacent in all that he'd accomplished just moments ago by making old things new again. Then he heard something. The door to Renee's room opened slightly and he heard the voice of a child, a little girl.

"Grandmere? Grandmere? Tu vas bien?"

The little girl walked over to her grandmother. When the jaundiced figured rolled over on its back with frozen dead eyes, the child screamed. The Horseman sighed with ennui. He was unmoved because it was a dramatic scene, he'd observed over, and over again...the hysterical discovery of a dead body by the living. And like the French countryside, it bored him.

"Not tonight, Monsieur. Not tonight."

Time to go, he thought as he headed for the window with his black cloak trailing behind him. Adults rushed into the room to remove the terrified little girl who'd just discovered the corpse of her eighty-nine year old grandmother. As people left the death room, one man remained behind. The horseman was rather surprised when his red eyes locked with the man in Renee's room.

He knew that the man saw him for what he was—*morte elegante*. He figured the silly bastard was probably taken aback by the long opera scarf wrapped around his bony neck, and the wide brimmed hat fashionably placed on his skull. The horseman was vain. Were it not for his red eyes, skeletal face and hands, why he could have been a minister! In a way he was, just a simple minister of death.

He heard the man whisper his real name, *Le Ankou*, as the man made the sign of the cross over himself. The specter threw his head back and laughed. The Ankou knew the tradition: if a living Breton could see and hear the traveling death specter, that person was not long for this world. Snickering, he watched beads of sweat dripping from the man's forehead. Even though the horseman was not due to return to Paimpont for several weeks to collect this spirit, he thought he'd have some fun with the trembling Frenchman. He cocked his sideways head and gave him a barbarous smile.

"There is room for one more on my cart," The Ankou hissed.

Then a gentle voice distracted him. As he looked out the window, The Ankou saw a young beautiful Renee stroking the necks of his gaunt, hollow eyed cart horses. She blew a kiss to the death spirit. He chuckled slightly, caught the kiss and blew it back to her. Then he whipped around and smirked fiendishly at the frightened man who fell to his knees before him, frantically muttering a prayer. Ever the gentleman, he politely doffed his hat and bent down to whisper in the man's ear with icy breath.

"Yes, I do have room for one more," The Ankou said softly. "But not tonight, Monsieur. Not tonight."

CARTERHAUGH 'S WELL

My father and I were small time quarterhorse breeders in Northern Colorado. Several years ago my father, Leon Darkhawk, and other members of the community sold our water rights to developers. We were fools. The money wasn't nearly enough, and quickly spent. My family and others on our Reservation were slowly losing our ability to maintain our horse farms. Our animals were dying. Perhaps this is what the developers wanted. Because they controlled the water, they controlled the land, and consequently our lives.

As I watched my favorite grey dying in the field, I felt my father's hand on my shoulder. The pattern was the same for each death. First, the horse dropped to its knees. Its eyes rolled backward and then the horse placed its muzzle in the dust. Once the animal rolled on its flank, it surrendered life with one final, painful gasp.

"I'll get my gun. We"ll get rid of them all at once. It will be better this way."

"No. I've heard there's a well on Carterhaugh land. Once I get there I'll figure out away to drag the horses there or bring water back."

"Yvonne, it's not our land, and it's dangerous. Nobody knows what's out in Carterhaugh land. Seasoned men won't even hunt up there. I forbid it."

"You can't stop me. I'm going, Dad."

Local historians were never able to quite figure when the Carterhaugh family arrived in the region. The earliest records indicated a James and Janet Carterhaugh and their two children arrived in the area sometime in the 1600's and they owned about 400 acres of land near the Ute Reservation. No one knew anything about the present day family. What everybody presumed is that Carterhaughs lived on the land somewhere, since posted signs forbade trepass across their property. Among the locals it was territory that had a reputation for strange occurrences. The elders in my tribe call it in the Shonshoni language, a place of the *deyaipe*, a place of the dead.

A month ago, a little boy from the Reservation got lost near Carterhaugh land. Five days later, the boy was returned on horseback and hastily deposited on the edge of the Reservation land by a horseman. Unharmed, the little boy seemed well nourished, happy and healthy. He didn't know how he came to Carterhaugh land, yet he spoke of the new friends he'd met, little children with beautiful green eyes. He didn't understand why his parents were upset. After all, he'd only been gone an hour or so. It was rumored that one of the elder women, a woman gifted with spirit sight, said that the man who delivered the boy was shamelessly handsome and not of this world. But when pressed for details, she couldn't exactly describe what he looked like. She did recall that he was a white man with fair skin and large green eyes, though.

Whoever the Carterhaughs were, they were better off than the Ute. No developers took their water rights, no developers could ever find them. It was as though the Rocky Mountains had cloaked their land in an invisible mist protecting them from the predators of progress.

"I won't let another one of our horses die. I'll travel by moonlight. I heard a spring rises at the edge of their land. I'll check it out tonight and be back before daybreak. And no, you can't come with me."

My father shook his head. "At least take my shotgun with you." Beneath the furrowed brow of tired rancher, came a sigh and a smile. "To protect you from any of the living."

#

That night the moon came full and white. This was the time to make my move. I had grown up around these parts and had always ridden around the edge of the woods. At night the trees whispered to me, and I would often hear the giggling and laughter of children. I wrote the laughter off as my imagination, but in my culture, others would have interpreted the giggling as haughty spirits, taunting the living. Quite frankly, I didn't believe in any of it, magic, good spirits or otherwise. Like my dad, I was a practical gal. If I ran into any "spirits" in the woods I didn't like, there was nothing a shot gun blast couldn't handle.

Fox, my trail horse, sees much more clearly in the dark. Most horses do. He trotted through the woods at a good pace. The forest's dark path had several twists and turns. Somehow I felt I was going in the right direction, although I wasn't sure. And then I saw the oasis, the water that would save my horses.

Through the clearing, the moon reflected in a large black mirror that was the spring. An owl lurking in a nearby tree swooped down and broke the still water. I dismounted and lead Fox to the water's edge. Quietly, he put his head down and drank. I was weary, but happy that my night's work was accomplished. I laid my gun down. At least one of my horses satisfied himself in the sweet dark waters on the Carterhaugh land. From out of nowhere there was a rush of wind, and a chill came over me.

"What woman dares to drink from my well?"

It was a man's deep voice. My horse lifted his head, turning to see the figure behind him. His eyes became as wide as saucers, and he snorted and pawed the ground nervously, his ears pasted flat against his head.

My back faced him. I knelt down and began to pick up the gun. If he tried anything, I would shoot. I looked for his reflection in the water, and saw nothing but the reflection of the moon. You can't shoot what you can't see. His line of sight was better than mine. If he shot first, my back faced him and I was finished.

"Don't even think about killing me. Turn and see me."

So I did.

He sat atop a milk white steed and wasn't a very big man. A cowboy hat, typical in these parts, was conspicuously absent. His hair was white blond, sleek and flowed slightly past his shoulders. He wore a strange kind of cloak made of buckskin, that looked tattered and handsewn in parts, and his eyes were a bright sea green.

His whole appearance was somewhat was out of place for Northern Colorado. He was almost medieval looking. Yet, still I wasn't afraid of him.

"How did you know I thought about killing you?"

"I could hear your thoughts in the wind."

"Yeah, right. So. You a Carterhaugh?"

"Yes. Why do you drink from my well?"

"My name is Yvonne Darkhawk and I'm from the Ute Reservation on the other side of these woods. My father and other ranchers sold their water rights to developers. Our horses are dying. They need more water than we can give them. That's why I'm here."

He shook his head. "You sold your water rights? How can you sell rights to something owned by the heavens? You are a Native American. You above all should understand that."

"What?"

Suddenly, I heard the familiar sound of children's laughter. It was almost musical. A soft green rolling mist drifted in our direction. I noticed the man looked uneasy.

"Get on your horse and leave here. Whatever you do, you mustn't look into the mist. Now go!" He turned his horse and galloped straight into the green fog.

I jumped on Fox's back and turned him into the direction which would take me home. The water must have invigorated him. He was energized and picked up a good pace. We raced through the woods back to my farm. I didn't turn back to look at the mist. For the first time in my life, I was truly frightened in a place that I had known so well. The children's laughter which had so often amused me now terrified me.

I barely got my horses settled in the barn, when lightheadedness overcame me. Something about my experience in the woods drained me, weakened me. But I knew that I would have to return to the spring. My work wasn't done quite yet.

#

I returned under the cover of night again. This time I brought Fox, a pregnant mare, and another older horse. I brought my Dad's shotgun again, but I just couldn't help thinking it would really be of no use on Carterhaugh land.

Fox knew the way to the well better than I did. When I reached the forest clearing, I saw the man with the white horse. He stood there...waiting for me.

"Hello. I hoped you'd return. Don't be afraid. Send your horses to the well."

I let the horses go and they headed straight for the water. "Who are you? What was that green mist?"

"Dismount your horse and sit with me by the spring. I'll tell you a story. You will find that the water has healing properties. Your horses will have good health from now on."

I wasn't sure if I should do this. But somehow I had this sense that he wouldn't hurt me. There was something about him, something both sad and sweet at the same time. I sat down next to him with the gun on the ground next to me.

"My name is Ian Carterhaugh. I am the last of the Carterhaugh men. James and Janet Carterhaugh, my parents came to this region in the 1600's."

"I thought the earliest settlers were Spanish colonists in this area. I'm sure you mean your *descendants* lived in this area in the 1600's."

"No, my family and I lived in this area."

"So you're four hundred years old?"

"About that, yes."

"Give me a break." Right about now, the shotgun seemed to be a real good idea again. The man was a psycho. I went to grab the shotgun again.

I was quick, he was faster. He grabbed my arm. "That won't do you any good. Listen to me!" His voice softened. "Please. You are native to these parts, you should understand what I am about to tell you." He sat down and guided me back to the ground and took the gun from my hands.

"Earth spirits control these woods. My original home was where your ranch is. My family was starving, so my father sent me hunting for food in these woods. As I was riding many centuries ago, I fell from my horse. I think I hit my head. When I awoke, I knew that I was in a strange land, where time stops, no one grows old, no one dies. I was in the land of water and wood spirits. Some people call us fairies."

"So you're a fairy?"

"Yes, but a part of me is still human. The Fairy Queen of these woods, Isilla, killed my family to trap me. She desires me to become immortal, like her." He sighed in disgust. "In that way, I could become her consort. But there is more. Every seven years, the fairies pay their tithe to hell with a human soul. It means that I must die in order to become as she is—an immortal. Do you believe what I am telling you?"

I felt suddenly speechless and stupid. "You know, I knew there was something strange about you."

"Yes. Your horses sensed it. We are creatures of the primordial earth, animals know this. We cannot hide from them."

His looks had completely taken me aback. What height he lacked, was made up by a wiry muscular frame. Ian had to be at least as old as me, about twenty eight or so. His eyes were a sea green, and his skin had the dewey radiance of youth. I thought he was looking pretty good for someone pushing four centuries.

"This is very hard to take. The only reason, I even remotely believe you is because this region has shrouded the Carterhaughs in mystery since I was little girl. Were there other people in your settlement? Where are they?"

"Dead, or in service to Isilla, along with many others that have gotten lost in these woods over the centuries. Those who are enslaved to Isilla may as well be dead. They would be better off. She draws out their life force and they become ghostly shells which she controls."

"Were you responsible for returning the Jackson boy?"

"Yes. I risked my own life to save his by leaving Carterhaugh

Woods. He was to be a sacrifice for Isilla, but instead I brought him home to his parents. He was just an innocent little boy who was fairy charmed. I traded my life for his; it was the right thing to do. But now my time has come."

"So, are you telling me that you will be next in line to die?"

He nodded. "It is time to pay our tithe to hell again. But you can save my life." Then he placed his hand on my cheek. "I feel the loneliness in your soul. Do you think you could love me, Yvonne Deerhawk? If you can, you must drink from the well and complete the tasks I ask of you. I know your soul. It called to me from the woods many, many years ago."

"I don't know if I can love anyone. This was too much to take. I'd been married once, but that relationship was a mistake. Love, or at least passion, was long gone. Death and sadness are the only things I really know."

Ian looked down. "I see. I made a mistake in choosing you as the one. I have to go and meet my fate. Please go and don't come back. It's too dangerous here."

The mist and green light started rolling in again. Then the children's laughter followed. But this laughter had a strange tone to it. It taunted me. Ian jumped on his horse and drove the animal straight into the mist as if to distract it from coming near me. I mounted Fox and quickly gathered the other horses. Danger was near.

#

When I returned at sunrise with my horses, my father was there waiting for me.

"Yvonne, I was worried sick. What happened?"

Suddenly I felt weak. "I don't know. But Dad look at the horses."

Fox, the mare and the old gelding were racing around their pasture like spring colts. I was amazed since it seemed only a few hours ago, their strength was fading. One drink from the Carterhaugh's Well had renewed their lives.

"Well, I'll be damned." My father scratched his head with amazement.

"See Dad? I told you the water would save them." The next thing I knew, I was in bed. Father put a moist compress on my head. I 'd collapsed from exhaustion. As I lay there, all I could think of was Ian, and the sad look in his eyes, when I told him that I didn't know if I could love anyone. But he *needed* me. At that moment, I made up my mind. I would try to save his soul.

#

There was no moonlight to guide me this time, but Fox's memory of the sweet tasting well water left the impression than I had hoped for. The old gelding found his way even under the cloak of darkness. When I arrived at the spring, Ian was there, standing beside his pool of water, gazing off into what should have been his own watery reflection. He didn't look at me at first.

"Yvonne, I did not think you would come back."

"I had to, Ian. I didn't have a choice."

"You will die if you do not succeed. Do you still want to do this?"

"Yes."

He turned around to face me and brought me to to the edge of the well. We knelt down on the ground. Ian leaned over and filled his cupped hands with water. "Drink, my love, drink from the well of the fairy." As I drank the cool sweet water, I heard his voice dreamily instructing me.

"Nothing can happen before All Hallow's Eve, when the veil between the worlds is thin. At midnight, a procession will rise up from the well, shrouded in the greenish mist of fairy. You will see many knights and other fairy folk before you see me. Some will be pleasing to the eye; some will not. Never look directly at the fairy folk or stare into the mist, as you can be charmed that way. Toward the end of the unearthly procession, you will see a knight on a black

41

horse, behind him a knight on a brown horse, and finally a knight on a white horse. Pull that rider down. It will be me. I can tell you no more than this: no matter what happens, do not let go of me or I will die and so will you. Can you do this?"

I drew him close to me, and his body felt like a warm safe haven. I cried as he wrapped his arms around me, and held me close. He whispered, "May I presume that the answer is yes?"

#

Three months had past and I stayed away from the spring and the woods. As each day drew closer to Fall, I yearned for Ian. It was a pleasant distraction from day to day farm chores. With the little water I had brought back, our horses were given a rebirth. But I was still worried a lot about my father. His spirits were not good and he didn't look well. I wanted to tell him that if we could just last a bit longer, things would be better after October 31st. I could feel it.

Halloween had finally arrived along with the signs of an earnest winter. During Halloween Day, local children came trick or treating from the Ute Reservation school. Around three o'clock in the afternoon, an assortment of characters appeared at my door. There were clowns, witches, Power Rangers, and one solitary little angel. One by one, they lined up in front of my door waiting for candy. The Angel was last in line.

She was an adorable study in pink lace with silvery gossamer wings sewn to her shoulders. She had a little paper crown that had been carefully dusted with glitter and spelled "Angel." As I handed her a candy bar, she looked up at me sweetly with big brown eyes. I thought that she was lovely...until the raspy voice of an old woman poured out of her mouth.

"Ye shall never have him," she hissed. "The man is mine and will be my consort before the dawn breaks."

I froze in my tracks. The little girl smiled at me. "Thank you, Ma'am. Happy Halloween!" The vicious little angel ran off

"Ye shall never have him."

and vanished into the crowds of trick-or-treating children, leaving me standing in the doorway, trying to catch my breath. Isilla gave me a warning. She would not let go of Ian easily.

#

As the sun set, I began my journey across the dark woods to Carterhaugh's Well. I dressed warmly for the journey because the spring was located at a higher altitude, and at this time of the year the area would be shrouded in snow. When I reached the well, it looked like a pristine white blanket with a huge watery black hole in its center.

Pine tree branches overshadowed the water. I stood quietly in the darkness behind a tree waiting for the procession of the dead. The hoot of an owl signaled the arrival of midnight. I took a breath and waited.

I heard a low rumbling coming from the earth, right before the center of the well opened up. The strange mist Ian warned me about poured outward from the center of the spring. I tried not to look at the wondrous mist and its images, keeping in mind what I was told. The mist was lead by a dancing green light that bounced in mid air keeping in sync with some invisible orchestra. Periodically, it would stop and the ball of light would stretch around as though it were glancing over its shoulder to make sure the unholy procession following it remained intact.

One by one the dead and the fairy came. Some of the females were beautiful-looking as though they had fallen from the canvas of a Pre-Raphaelite painting. But when I looked at the others, a chill overcame me. Each had an obvious physical imperfection, a cloven hoof, a skeletal hand, or one side of a face completely rotted away. I heard Ian's voice whisper to me through the darkness.

This is why they pay a tithe to hell. To maintain their physical beauty. If I die, their deformities will vanish again...for at least seven years.

Isilla's servants were reptilian creatures dressed in medieval clothing. Others were imps with twisted postures. The most terrifying of the bunch were emaciated human men, putrifactive animated corpses. My heart raced and my palms sweat as I watched each miserable creature pass by me.

Finally, the armored knights appeared. First, came the knight on the black horse. A spectre of death, he had no face. Long bony phalanges wrapped themselves around the horse's reins. His mount was a dead thing, too, with hollow eye sockets and sagging skin over its bones.

Just as Ian explained, the brown horse followed. Its rider was more human looking, but bore resemblance to someone who'd spent a good portion of his life battling some wasting disease. The knight was pale and weary as though life had been drained from him through centuries of pain.

Then came the rider on the white horse. It was my Ian. He had loose silver chains around his body and a long loose chain around his neck. Queen Isilla held the end of his chains in her hand as she drifted slowly through the tree branches. The fairy queen was an incredible sight, with long flowing hair. Her features were aquiline and her eyes, an electric green. She was as some beautiful flowers are in the field, lovely to look at but poisonous and deadly when touched.

I tried to conceal my slightest movements, but the snow crunched beneath my feet.

"Stop!" She hissed. "There is someone among us!"

The procession of the dead came to a halt. The faceless knight raised his head and like a wolf in search of blood, sniffed the air.

"Human blood is near. It is carried on the wind, Your Majesty." His dead voice croaked.

Queen Isilla was impatient. If Ian didn't die within the hour, she would have to pay the tithe to hell. Time was short.

"I see no one. Let us move on." The procession began again.

Now was my chance. I ran over to Ian and ripped him from his horse. His chains snapped off as we tumbled to the ground. For one second in time, I saw his pleading eyes.

Hold on. I beg you.

As soon as I had tightened my grip around him, he changed. His muscle softened in my hands and his skin was cold and slimey to the touch. He was shrinking. Seconds later, I held a slithering eel-like creature with bloody fangs that lunged at my neck. Then the eel grew warmer and warmer until it hurt to the touch. I nearly lost my grasp of him because Ian shapeshifted into a burning stick of wood. The flames seered my flesh, and the smell of my own burning skin made me sick to my stomach. But the pain! Oh, the pain! I couldn't bear it and thought I would surely die.

No matter what happened I held onto the burning wood even though I was in insufferable agony.

Please my love. Hold on. A soft voice whispered. *And try to keep me close.*

He had become a pile of leaves. Isilla raised her arms, laughing as she did so because she'd summoned the wind to disperse them. I dove into the pile and grabbed every leaf I could, holding them close to my heart. From there, the leaves became hot burning coals. Insane with the pain of having been burned before, I heard the coals speak to me.

Kiss me now or I will die.

I forced my face into the burning black coals. I was blind now from the fire and smoke. I smelled my hair burning and felt fire burning my brow and lashes. If I survived this ordeal, I would be permanently disfigured. But that didn't matter because I was dying.

I vaguely remember hearing wails rise from amongst the ranks. Ian explained that Carterhaugh's Well opened up as red flames spewed forth from a black hole in the center of the water. One by one the fairy creatures were sucked into the burning hole by some great force. The last one to enter the infernal portal was Queen Isilla herself.

But before she entered, she turned to Ian and screamed.

"Bastard! If I'd knew that you'd betray me, I'd have cut out

"She was as some beautiful flowers are in the field, lovely to look at, but poisonous and deadly when touched."

your heart of flesh and replaced it with one of stone!" Ian told me that two large claws reached out from the flames and pulled Isilla, now a wrinkled old woman, into the inferno. The well closed up and the water was still and black once more, reflecting only the light of the moon.

He carried me over to the well and dipped me in the water. My burns healed and when he kissed my lips, they were also healed. My sight was restored, and Ian stood naked before me. We made love, and my soul as well as my body was finally healed.

#

No one in the tribe ever asked where this strange white man came from. Ian gave our tribe his land and rights to all natural resources existing on it. We no longer needed to bargain back our water rights from seedy developers. My father welcomed Ian into our family as I had welcomed him into my heart.

Carterhaugh Woods will always be a mystery to me. But now when Ian and I ride through forest in the moonlight, the woods are peaceful...and wonderfully silent.

AGGI THE GO - BETWEEN

Kelly O' Hara knocked at the door on apartment 7B in an old building on 17 Orchard Street. The first raps were polite, but as her desperation increased she pounded on the door with a clenched fist.

"Open up! I know you're in there. Please answer. I'm begging you."

She heard the sound of feet shuffling across a floor. Then Kelly heard the sounds she had longed to hear: a series of deadbolts and chain locks becoming undone. The door opened a crack, and a large, glassy-looking, single blue eye stared at her.

"And you are?" A voice asked.

"Kelly. Kelly O'Hara. I'm a friend of Mary— "

"Yeah, I know Mary Tortariccio."

"Did she tell you I would be coming? Will you see me?"

"Well," the voiced replied, "I guess you ain't goin' away if I don't. C'mon in."

Kelly sighed with relief as the door opened all the way. Once she saw a full frontal view of Mrs. Aggi Mezzano. Her heart sank.

Mrs. Mezzano was a slight woman with a hunched back. One arm was significantly shorter than the other. She a head of tight grey pin curls, and stogie dangled out of the side of her mouth. Her right eye, abnormally large and made from glass, clearly failed to compliment the more normal looking left eye. She walked with a limp, had a few teeth, none of which were neighbors, and waxy red, cupid's bow lips painted on her upper lip. She smelled of mothballs. The woman frightened her, but what choice did she have? Desperate times call for desperate measures. Kelly swallowed. No matter who or what Aggi Mezzano was, she would just suck it up and be nice.

"Aw c'mon. Don't let the looks scare ya," she smiled. "All of us go-betweens look like this. It ain't easy bringing happiness and love to lonely women. And besides like I always say, ugly women need love, too. In my day, I had lotsa men. So let's talk. Come in and cop a squat." Kelly nodded and followed Aggi as she gestured her to a beat up kitchen table.

"Thank you." Kelly entered the apartment and sat down. She saw an old Mickey Mouse clock on the kitchen wall. Mickey said it was only ten o'clock in the morning. She had been in Mrs. Mezzano apartment only for a minute, and yet it seemed like an hour had gone by.

"Wanna a glass of vino, Sweetie?" the old woman asked.

"No thank you. It's a little too early for wine."

"Well, don't mind me. Must five o'clock somewhere." She filled a juice glass with red wine, downed it one gulp, punctuating the act with a loud belch.

Ohmigod, I'm in the house of a gimpy, drunken, one-eyed, hunchback. It's all because that bastard left me for another woman, she thought.

"So lemme guess. You're about forty, right?" Mrs. Mezzano cocked her head. "You have two children, both girls. How nice. You got dumped for a much younger woman, right?"

Kelly felt blood rushing to her face. "How did you know that?"

"Like the banks these days, I like to know my customer. Let's face it. You can't cash a damn check without two hundred pieces of identification. The only thing you and I got between us is one mutual friend and a buncha words. Now let's get down to business. I want to know truth." Aggie drew herself up. "Look me in the eye."

Kelly glared at the burgeoning blue glass eye. "Yes?"

"The other eye." Mrs. Mezzano lifted her chin with her two fingers. "Yes, I see. Now talk. You come to see me about love or revenge? Answer quickly!"

"What?"

51

"You come to see me about love or revenge? Answer quickly."

"You heard me. Love or revenge. Which is it?"

"Love! I mean, I want to, I'm really, I'd like to meet at man. I'm very lonely since Evan decided to leave me and —" Kelly burst into tears, barely getting the words out. Mrs. Mezzano hobbled over to the couch and grabbed Kelly's hand.

"The first efforts in finding true love is to let go of the past, if you can't do that, I can't help you. Are you ready to surrender your pain?"

"Yes," she whispered.

"Oh good. Now that all the sensitivity crap's over with, let's get to work. Lemme get a pen, I need a pen. Hold on." The old woman shuffled into the kitchen and began digging through a broken kitchen drawer. She returned with an old quill pen, a jar of red ink, a beat up leather bound book, and a yellowed envelope.

Kelly winced. She wondered if the old girl intended to make her sign a pact with the devil and her new boyfriend would have a set of horns and a tail. "You know, Mrs. Mezzano, Mary is very happy with the new husband she has. She says that she owes it all to you. Her last husband was horrible to her."

"Call me Aggi. And while I'd like to take credit for the whole ball o' wax, people have to make their own happiness. And love ain't never perfect either, especially when you get around our age. You know what I mean, the face gets jowly, the boobs sag, the belly hangs. Nothing is worse than a low slung butt."

The thought that Aggi and Kelly were even remotely the same age made Kelly nauseous. She just turned forty. Aggi could have been seventy or seven hundred. Kelly couldn't tell, but no way were they sharing the same birth decade.

"Aggi, what is it that you do? Introductions? Do you host parties? How will you have me meet men?"

"No, they come to you. You tell me what you want and I send them to you. You like, you pick. You no like, you call me and pick somebody else. First, you gotta sign a contract. Mark an 'X' right here where it says 'the party of the first part, etc.' "

Kelly looked at the back of the blank envelope. "There's

nothing written down. It's just an old envelope. I'm not signing that. It's a blank envelope."

"Oh I can see this is not going to be easy." Aggi's real eye looked upward. "You are really going to make me work this one, huh?" Thunder cracked outside after she finished speaking.

"I really don't want strangers coming to my house."

"Strangers are just friends we don't know."

"But what if the person is some kind of a maniac? Can't we do this another way?"

"Well, I supposed you could meet him in a public place. I normally don't do this, but since you're Mary's friend, I'll help you out. Now tell me. What kind of man do you want?"

Kelly closed her eyes. *A Rudolph Valentino. Some one virile, yet sensitive. He must be tall and well built, a formidable man. Someone who can walk into a boardroom of a major corporation and command respect, yet a sensitive man who will help me hang red velvet drapes. And appearances matter. I spent too many years living with the village slob. I want a handsome man*, she thought.

She opened her eyes. "Aggi, looks don't matter and so long as he's nice, that counts more." She gave her best smile thinking the old woman would be impressed with her faux sincerity.

Instead, Aggi rose from her chair. With a crackly voice, she began to warble as she waltzed across the room. " 'I'm the Shei-i-k of Araby, your love belongs to me-e-e.' Song came out in 1921. Heard it in a Speakeasy once. Good times, back then good times."

"Huh?"

Aggi whipped around and pointed a bony finger at her.

"Stop lying to me, young lady. I'm old not stupid. You don't want someone who's *nice*. No woman wants a nice man in their deepest fantasies. You want a man's man," she said raising her hand and making two small circles with her thumb and forefinger, "But he's gotta be sweet and hang your kitchen curtains."

Kelly brushed a wisp of blond hair that fell lightly across her brow. "That's exactly what I thought. You read my mind. Is that possible?"

54

"I'm the Sheik of Araby, your love belongs to me."

"Whether reading your mind or helping you find the man of your dreams, I am a full service go-between. Just put your faith in Aggi Mezzano. Now be at the diner at seven o'clock tonight. Oh, and you'll need this." She handed her a small purple sachet. "Sprinkle this on your bed right before you go out tonight. It's deer's tongue, and lavender. "

"Not a *real* deer's tongue?"

"It's a plant, honey, just a plant."

"Who will I be meeting? Who is he? Who will bring him?"

"Hoo-hoo-hoo, you sound like an owl." Aggi winked with her good eye. "No worries. Just go to the Forum Diner for dinner like you've been doing for the past coupla weeks. Must be lonely eating all by yourself. I know I hate eating by myself."

"How did you know *that*?" Kelly asked.

Aggi gave her a snaggle tooth grin. "I been around the block a turn or two."

#

Promptly at seven, Kelly entered the doors of the Forum Diner, a large North Jersey eatery on Route 4 in Paramus, New Jersey. By the time she was on her third cup of bitter brewed coffee, she realized that she had just made an idiot out of herself. Why did she do it? Why did she show up at the house of some crazy woman who claims to be a professional matchmaker? What was she thinking? She signaled her server for a check.

A perky little waitress ran over to her table and looked as though she was about to burst. "Excuse me, Ma'am. There's a man here looking for a single woman named Kelly. Is that you?"

"I'm Kelly. Who wants to see me?"

"He does." She pointed over to a man dressed in a burnoose. Kelly felt her heart pounding. He was 6'2" with gorgeous smoldering deep set eyes hidden beneath his hooded cloak. His hair was slicked down and parted in the middle. Dressed like an Arabic sheik, the man would have been completely laughable were he not so devastatingly handsome. All she heard in her head was the off key refrain of the Sheik of Araby being sung by Aggi, over and over again. Female diner patrons sighed and stared at him with vacant smiles on their faces as this big muscular hunk walked over to her table and sat down across from her.

"Hello. I understand you were looking for Rodolfo Valentino," he said ever so seriously. "Am I not right?"

"Well, not in the literal sense." Kelly listened carefully to his words and blushed. He had a slight Italian accent and she was intrigued. "Did Aggi send you?"

He cocked his head. "Aggi? Who is this Aggi? Ah, *si*, you mean Agrippina? Yes, she suggested we meet. She said that you were interested in romantic love." He reached over and kissed her hand. "I brought you something." From some place deep inside his burnoose he produced a bouquet of flowers.

"White tea roses, my favorite." As Kelly took the flowers, her stomach quivered. "Thank you. So please tell me about yourself. Like why are you dressed in a costume?"

He grabbed her hand, and a warm shock wave went through her body. "I did it for you. I'm what you asked for. I have an MBA from the Wharton School, and I'm a Vice President in Charge of Finance for a technology company. I like poetry, music and dance. And I like rich red velvet drapes. My name is Rodolfo."

This is just too weird. I have to get out of here, she thought.

"Listen, I'm not feeling comfortable about this. In fact, this isn't me. I mean this is really not me. So I should go." Kelly threw down money for the check and the tip and bolted out of the diner, leaving Rodolfo the Sheik mystified and alone at the Forum Diner.

#

When she pulled into her driveway, she turned off the engine and placed her head on the steering wheel. She was both sad and furious.

57

Why would someone who looked like that want someone like me? Why did I ever go see that crazy fortuneteller in the first place?

By the time she placed her key in the door lock, her phone was ringing off the wall. Aggi was on the line.

"So what was the matter with Rudy? He liked you. Handsome brute, right?"

She cleared her throat. "Yes, but Aggi, he showed up dressed in a costume. It was embarrassing."

"Ya know, kid. You I don't get. And I can't get the hell outta here and move on until you're happy. Once and for all, what do you want?"

"First off, I'm not a kid. And what are you talking about? Where are you going? You're not running from the law are you? Are you on the lam?"

"Never you mind my troubles." Aggi sighed with disgust. "Okay, maybe the latin lover ain't your type. I know. You need someone more refined, like an Englishman with one of them highbrow accents. What about that? Fresh outta guys from the Emerald Isle right now. You know, the other go-between Mrs. Finnerty usually handles you Irish gals, but she's in Dublin attending a wedding. One of her success stories I might add."

"I don't know." Kelly paused for a minute. "I think I've lost my mind. I mean listen to me. I'm talking to a complete stranger about my love life. It's embarrassing, it's pathetic, I'm pathetic."

Aggi completely ignored the statement. "Just sprinkle your bed with the lavender and deer's tongue and call me in the morning. Alrighty, you got it, a sophisticated Englishman *it is*. Now goo' bye." She slammed the phone down.

#

Although Kelly didn't know why, she felt compelled to sprinkle the sachet across her sheets. What did she have to lose? The lavender was a little overpowering at first, but as she closed

58

her eyes, she found that its scent had an incredibly soothing effect. Despite a nervous resistance, a deep dreamless sleep came over her. She felt completely at rest— until she felt a man kissing her neck and whispering into her ear.

"Hello, darling." A large hand caressed her arm from her shoulder all the way down to her fingertips.

"Omigod!" She fumbled for her night table in the dark. She remembered that her ex-husband kept a revolver hidden in it. As she poked about blindly, she heard a man's soft laughter. She found the gun, jumped from the bed, and flipped the light switch. Aggi had done it again.

Kelly had to hand it to the old girl. She knew how to pick good looking men, the type that were straight out of bodice ripping romance novels. There was a tall, very elegant, 19th century man in a grey mourning coat with an ascot and a walking stick laying in the bed. A beaver top hat covered shoulder length black hair. He had piercing blue eyes, and overall a charming, roguish look. She noticed that he fit every inch of his suit rather well. Nevertheless, she pointed the gun straight at his chest.

"You move and I'll shoot. My ex-husband was a cop and I know how to use this."

Instead of anger, his face broke into a broad smile. "My darling, you needn't do that. I am not here to hurt you. I am here to love you, and to make love to you."

"Yes, but your some kind of a spirit. You're evil."

"Well, not all of us are necessarily evil." He said shifting his eyes and looking at his curled fingers as though he was inspecting a manicure. "Admittedly, some of us still are."

"So what are you and Aggi? Demons?"

"Neither." He stood up and outstretched his arms to her. "Put the gun down. Let's talk. I promise, you'll feel much better, my dear."

"How about I stand here and you talk. Do you have a name?"

"Yes, Dorian Grey. Care to see to my portrait?"

"Not interested!" Kelly shrieked. How was she going to get rid of this man-thing, whatever he was. She felt panicked. "Tell me about Aggi."

"Ah, yes. *Agrippina the Younger*. How familiar are you with the history of ancient Rome?"

"I had one course in high school. What's your point?"

"Aggi, as you call her, is Agrippina the Younger. She was a beautiful woman thousands of years ago, but she lived a debauched life, murdered innocents and produced a crazy son, Nero, who eventually killed her. Well, God punished her for all her evil deeds. Her beauty was taken away, and she was denied entrance to paradise. For centuries she's been an old hag, doomed her walk the Earth until she brings love and happiness to women, making up for her mortal life's misdeeds. She became *Agrippina Il Mezzano*, Aggi the Go-between, the matchmaker. Many of these 'Aggi' types walk the Earth. In Spain, they are *los casamenteros*, in Italy? *I mezzani*. In Germany? *Die Ehestifter*. Once a go-between repays her debt, she moves on."

"And what if things don't work out?"

"She'll be here for another thousand years trying to make the lovelorn happy. Sort of a permanent Purgatory if you will."

Dorian rose from the bed and faced her. Finger by finger, he carefully removed the gun from her hand. It fell to the floor. Then he placed his hands on her shoulders. "You are Agrippina's last stop."

"So what do you want me to do about it?"

"Let me make you happy. Then Aggi can get her wings and go on."

"I don't care about Aggi's wings. For once in my life I care about someone else. Me!"

Instead of responding to the remark, he scooped her up in his arms. He placed his lips over hers. Her body responded. She started removing his mourning coat and rubbing her hands up and down his body. She felt the curve of every muscle in his arms and shoulders. He ran a long kiss across her neck. She sighed. She had

60

not caressed or kissed a man like this in years. Kelly felt as though she were outside of her body and relished every moment in this man's arms, until she felt a strange protuberance in an area where it shouldn't have been. She opened her eyes.

During the course of their passionate foreplay, the top hat fell from his head. Protruding between his shiny locks of black hair were two small horns, the kind found on the head of a baby goat. Kelly backed away from him.

"Stay away from me. You're some kind of demon sent from hell to torture me."

"No," he replied, "that would have been your ex-husband. Come back to arms, lovey. Don't deny me." Dorian started walking towards Kelly.

Her eyes scoured the floor for the gun and she reached it. It would be like one of those old Superman televisions shows from the Fifities. First, she would shoot him. Then, if by some chance he was still standing, which was more than likely since he wasn't human anyway, she would fling the gun at him as she ran out the door. The whole act was probably useless, but Kelly wasn't going down without a fight.

She pulled the trigger, and dumped the entire cylinder of bullets into him. The series of shots pushed him back and he fell against a wall. He laughed as his body slid down the wall without any blood spatter. "See what you've done, poppet? You've killed me. O-o-o-h," he moaned. For a second, he tilted his head to one side and rolled back his eyes, and looked dead.

Kelly put the gun down and ran over to Dorian's crumpled body. "Oh, I'm so sorry! I've never killed anyone, once a bunch of beetles who were eating my vegetables, Omigod! What have I done?" She reached out to touch his face. "Dorian?"

In one swoop he grabbed her hand. She screamed and he taunted. "Naughty girl. Why did you try to shoot me? All I desire is to be your servant of love."

"Leave me alone." Out of nothing but sheer desperation, she grabbed a little sachet of deer's tongue, and lavender. There were a

"She dumped the herbs in her hand and blew them in Dorian's face."

few pieces of herbs remaining. When she picked it up, she noticed that Dorian had a panicked look across his face.

"Poppet, put that down. Think of Aggi, please. You don't know what you're doing. You don't want to hurt me."

Kelly shook her head. She dumped the herbs into her hand and blew them into Dorian's face. As she did this, his image began to fade until he vanished in front of her eyes. She felt the empty sachet bag grow full in her hand.

"Great, I've heard of men made of straw, but not men made of deer's tongue and lavender." She flung herself across the bed and wondered how everything got so crazy. Loneliness makes women do strange things, grow desperate, and try anything. Kelly decided to give up. She would never have another man in her life. Aggi had been right about one thing. She was too fearful for a man's love and she couldn't let go of the past. Maybe Rudolf and Dorian were just symbols, but they were symbols of what she feared the most: passion. Kelly walked over to the window. She open the little sachet bag, and released its contents to the wind. It was time to let go of fear. Maybe she wouldn't meet someone tomorrow or the next day, but when the time came she would be ready.

The doorbell rang. *Oh great. I wonder who it is now? Casanova? Julius Cesar? Atilla the Hun*? Kelly took a deep breath. "Who is it?"

"Ma'am? I'm Matthew Strickland your new next door neighbor. I just moved in. Sorry for calling on you so late, but I was worried. I thought I heard gunshots coming from here. I wanted to see if everything was okay."

Trembling, Kelly opened the door. A tall man wearing a black cowboy hat and tight fitting jeans stood quietly on her front steps. He had light hair and soft beckoning eyes. She hoped that Aggi didn't decide to send Doc Holliday over to court her. When he politely removed his hat, she stared at his head looking for protruding horns .

"Hi. I, uh, had the television on real loud. I was a watching an old John Wayne movie. You know, cowboys and Indians? I'm sorry if it was too loud."

"Not a problem. I'm retired law enforcement so I recognize gunshot sounds. But I guess it was just my imagination." He smiled. "Maybe I'm being a little forward here, but would you like to have a cup of coffee sometime? I'm new to the area."

Kelly sighed. "Sure. Why not? Just let me know when."

#

Six months later, Kelly found herself deliriously happy with one Matthew Strickland, a retired Texas Ranger. She asked him to drive her over to 17 Orchard Street, apartment 7B. Kelly asked Matthew to wait in the car while she ran in to check on an "elderly friend."

Just as Kelly was about to knock on the Aggi's door, another apartment door opened up and a cheerful old lady poked her head out. "If you're looking for Aggi, she's gone. Been gone for about six months now. Left no forwarding address. Said she was finally retiring. She was a strange old gal, but pretty nice."

"Thank you." Kelly looked at the door again and noticed a small sticker of a smiling angel with large oversized wings flying upward. The little angel held book in its hand entitled, "Move On, Dearie."

Kelly smiled and whispered, "I did Aggi, I did."

Aunt Elsie
1914~2002

www.ingramcontent.com/pod-product-compliance
Lightning Source LLC
Chambersburg PA
CBHW020646130626
46552CB00003B/1419